*A story for Tomás*

First published in Great Britain in 2002 by Brimax,
an imprint of Octopus Publishing Group Ltd
2-4 Heron Quays, London E14 4JP

© Octopus Publishing Group Ltd

A CIP catalogue record for this book is available
from the British Library.

ISBN 1 85854 483 1

Printed in China

# Little Duck
## on the
# Moon

Written and illustrated by Mark Burgess

BRIMAX

It was a wild and windy morning. Little Duck wanted to go out to look for her breakfast but she didn't like the wind one bit. She waited and waited, but the wind just kept on blowing.

"I shall have to go out," said Little Duck at last, for she was very hungry. She stepped cautiously out of her nest, but at that very moment a furious gust of wind swept Little Duck right off her feet and up into the air.

"Help!" she cried. Little Duck tried to fly back down to the ground, but the strong wind carried her higher and higher, tossing her round and round until she was quite dizzy.

In no time at all, she was above the clouds, drifting further and further
from the world below. The pond and trees grew smaller and smaller,
until Little Duck could not see them at all.

Suddenly, she began to fall. But Little Duck didn't fall back towards the blue earth – she fell towards the moon.

Little Duck landed on the moon with a bump. She picked herself up, shook off the moon-dust, and wondered what to do next. There did not seem to be any ponds on the moon.

Just then, Little Duck heard a "toot toot" behind her. She turned
around to see the Man in the Moon and his dog, Wigwag.

"Hello," said the Man in the Moon. "For a moment we thought you
were a broken promise."

"I'm not a broken promise. I'm Little Duck," she said. "And I don't know how I shall ever get home again. It looks too far to fly."

"Well, we'll worry about that later," said the Man in the Moon. "First let's go and have some breakfast. Then we've got twenty-three rainbows to make from all of these broken promises."

At the mention of breakfast, Little Duck remembered how hungry she was. She jumped straight into the Man in the Moon's car. The back of the car was full of broken promises, soft and shiny and all different colours.

"Where do the broken promises come from?" she asked.

"From the blue earth," explained Wigwag.

"That's where I'm from, too," said Little Duck.

When they got home,
the Man in the Moon
made breakfast.

"There, toast and honey.
What could be better?"
he said, putting a plate
in front of Little Duck.

"Thank you," said Little Duck
politely, but the toast was too
hard for her to eat, so she just
licked off the honey. When
the Man in the Moon wasn't
looking, Little Duck slipped
the slice of toast under her
wing, as she didn't want to
offend him.

"Goodness, have you finished already?" said the Man in the Moon,
and he gave Little Duck another slice of toast. She slipped that discreetly
under her other wing.

After breakfast, Wigwag and the Man in the Moon set to work making rainbows, stitching the broken promises together with fine thread.

"What are the rainbows for?" asked Little Duck.

"They are for the blue earth," explained Wigwag, "so that there will be hope in the world."

Wigwag and the Man in the Moon worked hard and at last the rainbows were finished. Wigwag tied on the labels.

"I know," exclaimed the Man in the Moon. "We'll send you back home on a rainbow!"

"We'll need an extra one," said Wigwag, "and we've no more broken promises."

"Then we'll go and find some more," said the Man in the Moon. "Little Duck, be sure to look out for the Squeakies while we are gone. Otherwise, they'll sneak in and snatch the rainbows."

When Wigwag and the Man in the Moon had gone, Little Duck did her best to watch out for the Squeakies. But it had been a very busy morning and her eyes kept closing. She had just dozed off when squeaky laughter woke her up with a start.

"Stop!" shouted Little Duck. "Stop! You mustn't take the rainbows!
You mustn't – or there will be no hope in the world."

But the Squeakies took no notice. They were running for the door.
Little Duck saw that her only chance was to get there before them.
She jumped up and ran across the table as fast as she could. Then, with a
tremendous leap, she landed at the door just in front of the Squeakies.

"Stop!" shouted Little Duck, spreading out her wings to bar the way. As Little Duck lifted up her wings, out fell the pieces of toast. The Squeakies stopped in their tracks.

Dropping the rainbows, they sniffed the toast and then they began to nibble at it. Soon they had gobbled up both slices, and ran off giggling.

"Were those the Squeakies?" asked the Man in the Moon, who had just returned. "Thank goodness they didn't take the rainbows! Well done, Little Duck."

"I think they just wanted some breakfast," said Little Duck. "Maybe if you leave out toast for them, they'll leave your rainbows alone."

Soon Little Duck's rainbow was finished. The Man in the Moon wrote a special label for it and Wigwag tied it on. Then they carried all the rainbows outside. The Man in the Moon lifted each rainbow into the air and let it float gently away towards the beautiful blue earth.

Little Duck balanced herself on top of the last rainbow and held on tight. The Man in the Moon lifted up the rainbow and gave it a little push as he let go.

"Bye, bye," said the Man in the Moon and Wigwag.

"Goodbye," said Little Duck. "And thank you."

Little Duck's rainbow floated slowly away from the moon towards the earth. As it drifted down, the rainbow slowly grew larger and larger, shimmering with all different colours. Soon it was a huge arch and Little Duck was just a tiny speck on the top.

When the clouds parted, Little Duck could see familiar green fields and woods far below. As she got closer, she saw the pond where she lived at one end of the rainbow.

Little Duck flapped her wings a few times, then she slid down the rainbow and splashed into the pond. Happily, she bobbed under the water to wash off the moondust. Then Little Duck ate her breakfast at last.

When Little Duck looked up into the sky again, she saw that the rainbow had disappeared. But Little Duck knew that her friends on the moon would be busy making more, to give the whole world hope.